Louisa on Screen

For Holly Standfast

RED FOX BALLET BOOKS
1. Little Swan
2. Louisa's Secret
3. Louisa in the Wings
4. A Rival for Louisa

A Red Fox Book

Published by Random House Children's Books
20 Vauxhall Bridge Road, London SW1V 2SA

A division of The Random House Group Ltd
London Melbourne Sydney Auckland
Johannesburg and agencies throughout the world

Text © Adèle Geras 2001
Illustrations © Karen Popham 2001

1 3 5 7 9 10 8 6 4 2

Printed and bound in Great Britain
by Bookmarque Ltd, Croydon, Surrey

Papers used by The Random House Group Limited are natural, recyclable products made
from wood grown in sustainable forest. The manufacturing processes conform to the
environmental regulations of the country of origin.

THE RANDOM HOUSE GROUP Limited Reg. No. 954009

www.randomhouse.co.uk

ISBN 0 09 941762 6

RED FOX BALLET BOOKS

Louisa on Screen

by Adèle Geras

illustrated by Karen Popham

RED FOX

Chapter One

My little sister Weezer was supposed to be helping me to pack for our holiday but, instead, she was moaning. She's very good at that, and she moans at me more than anyone else. It's as if she expects me to be able to do something about it.

"But Annie," she said. "It's not fair. I'm going to miss the dancing display. Miss Matting says it's the highlight of the whole year, and I won't be in it. *And* I was going to be the Sunshine Fairy."

"You look more like the Thunder Fairy at the moment, Weezer!" I said, trying to cheer her up. I'm ten, which is three years older than she is, and I'm always trying to cheer her up.

"*Louisa*!" said Weezer, looking crosser than ever.

"Sorry," I said. She decided some time ago that Weezer wasn't a suitable name for a ballet dancer, but I've called her Weezer for nearly eight years, and it's difficult to stop. She was standing by our dressing table, pointing her toes and lifting her leg up in a half-hearted sort of way. Round her neck she was wearing a pink scarf made of wispy, see-through material, which Mrs Posnansky, our neighbour, had given her as a going-away present.

Mrs Posnansky is Russian, and very old. Her own mother was a dancer when she was young and Mrs Posnansky believes Weezer is going to be a famous ballerina when she grows up. The two of them are great friends because this is what my sister thinks as well. She's mad about ballet, and whenever she stands still for more than a few seconds, she starts doing something like dance steps with her feet.

"Most people," I said, "would think that going off to Florida with their dad and staying in a posh hotel and swimming in a pool and visiting Disneyland and flying in an aeroplane was the most brilliant thing in the whole world."

"Why couldn't we go after the display?" Weezer asked.

"You know why," I said. "We've been over and over it. This was the only time Dad could take off work. And this is the only time the hotel wasn't booked up. You know all this."

Weezer had one arm above her head by now. Arms, she'd often told me, are almost as important in ballet as feet. She brought it down again, and flung herself backwards on to the bed.

"I know," she said. "But still . . . it's not fair. Phoebe's going to dance the Sunshine Fairy and I'm not. Phoebe's always taking my parts. Look what happened at Christmas when I couldn't be in the *Nutcracker* and she danced my role."

Phoebe is Weezer's best friend, and she's also very good at ballet. Weezer works hard making sure she's even better than Phoebe, and worrying in case she isn't.

"You'd twisted your ankle!" I said. "Even Darcey Bussell can't dance with a twisted ankle. And just remember, Miss Matting chose you first for the part. That must mean she thinks you're the best dancer."

Weezer managed a tiny smile. "It must, mustn't it?"

"Of course. And we'll have nearly a whole week with Dad."

"Yes," said Weezer. "That's true. That'll be ace."

Our dad and mum are divorced, and even though we see Dad quite a lot and phone him almost every day, he's not there all the time, and Weezer and I always long for the summer holidays when we can be with him properly, for a few days at least.

"You've hardly helped me with the packing at all. Your stuff is still all over the place," I said. "And now it's nearly time to go over to Tony's. You promised him you'd say goodbye. I'm coming too."

"I'll pack later," Weezer said. "Anyway, why are you coming? You don't usually come to Tony's."

"I just am," I said. "So there."

Tony lives next door to us. He's Weezer's friend, and when he first moved in she'd bullied him into dancing with her. Now he's almost as ballet-mad as she is.

She raced down the stairs and jumped over Bradman, our cat, who was curled up on the bottom step.

"Bye, Mum," she called out over her shoulder.

"Don't be late, girls," said Mum,

coming out of the kitchen. "You've got a long flight tomorrow."

She winked at me, and I winked back at her, but Weezer was halfway down the front path by this time, and didn't notice.

Tony opened the door almost as soon as we'd knocked on it.

"I'm here!" said Weezer. "Were you waiting behind the door?"

Tony blushed and said, "No, I was just passing . . . that's all. Come into the lounge."

"Why can't we go into the kitchen? We always go there first. Or to your room."

Weezer, I knew, was hoping for some cake. She liked cakes, and Tony's mum always seemed to have one standing on the kitchen table whenever we went round there.

"We'll go in the kitchen later," said Tony. "Come on."

Weezer opened the door of the lounge. "Why is it so dark in here, Tony?" she said,

and as she spoke, Tony turned on the lights – and Weezer shrieked. Shouts of "Surprise! Surprise!" came from every corner of the room.

"Oh!" Weezer put her hands over her mouth. "Phoebe! And Maisie ... and Tricia! How lovely! Have you all come to say goodbye to me?"

"It was my idea," said Phoebe.

"But I said we should have it at my house," Tony added.

Weezer was bright red in the face by now. "I'm only going to be away for a few days," she said. "People don't usually have a party just for going on holiday."

"But you're going to miss the dancing display," said Phoebe, "and we all know how sad you are about that. So we thought you could do your Sunshine Fairy dance for all of us, and then we'll do our bits. It would be like a rehearsal . . ."

"I've got a tape with the right music on it," said Tony. "The machine is all ready."

Weezer looked worried. "I'll have to go and get my ballet shoes from next door," she said.

"That's OK," said Phoebe. "We'll put our own shoes on while we wait."

Weezer danced her Sunshine Fairy dance, and everyone clapped.

"Thank you," she said. "I'll think of all of you on the day, I promise."

After Weezer's dance, everyone else went through their routines and then Tony said at last, "Come on. Let's go and get some cake and orange juice."

Weezer linked arms with Phoebe and smiled. "No one's ever thought of having a surprise party for me before," she said. "And I've never been to a party where I got to dance."

I could see she was feeling really happy. She smiled at Tony and said, "It's really nice of you to have a party for me! Thanks so much."

Weezer and Phoebe led the way out of the lounge.

When Phoebe's mum came to pick her up, she said to Weezer, "I'll miss you, Louisa. It won't be the same having a dancing display without you there. I wish you could be in it, I really do."

"I'll miss you, too. I'll send you a postcard. Make sure Miss Matting doesn't forget to make a video . . . Oh, how I wish

I could stay and be in it with everyone!"

Weezer was starting to frown again.

"Have a lovely holiday," said Phoebe and ran to her mum's car. Weezer waved till she was out of sight.

Chapter Two

Mum had given Weezer and me a rucksack each to take on holiday with us. Mine was bright blue with black straps and Weezer had chosen a pink and silver one. When I'd finished putting my notebook and felt-tipped pens and some books to read into mine, I glanced over to see what Weezer was taking. First, she put in a practice leotard, and then she wrapped her ballet shoes in a plastic bag and put them in too.

"You won't need those in Florida," I said.

She stared at me and sighed. "Ballet dancers," she explained patiently, "need ballet shoes. We have to practise every single day, come what may. Mrs Posnansky says her mother practised even when there were bombs falling, during the war."

"D'you even have to practise on holiday?"

"Yes, of course." She said it as though I was being really stupid, and maybe I was.

All the way over on the plane Weezer was as good as gold. She hardly moaned at all. After we landed in America, we drove to the hotel, which was called the Flamingo Palace. We could see the swimming pool through the plate glass windows of the lobby and when Weezer saw how big and blue it was, her mouth dropped open and she said, "Wowsers and double wowsers!"

(This was the best thing Weezer could ever say about anything.) "Can we go swimming straight away?"

Dad winked at me when Weezer wasn't looking, as if to say, I don't think we'll be hearing too much about ballet from now on. He was wrong of course.

I woke up very early on the first day we were in America. It was only six o'clock in the morning in Florida, but my body thought it was still at home, where it was nearly lunch time. What could I possibly do till it was time for breakfast? I looked over at Weezer's bed to see whether she was awake. Maybe I could get her to play cards with me or something. Or maybe we could play a pretend game. I blinked. Weezer wasn't in her bed at all! I got up and went to look in the bathroom. There was no sign of Weezer there either. Could she have got frightened in the night and got up and gone to find Dad? His room was next door to ours. I sat on my bed and wondered what to do. Dad wouldn't be too happy if I woke him up for nothing. Then I noticed that Weezer's pyjamas were lying on the floor beside her bed. Suddenly I felt cold all over. Where could she possibly be? Had she run away? I decided I had to wake Dad up after all and tell him she'd disappeared.

I ran out of the room without even bothering to put my slippers on. Then I glanced down the corridor and saw her. She was right down at the other end of it, near the lift, which was called the 'elevator' in America.

She was dressed in her practice leotard and ballet shoes, and I could see, even from where I was, that she was going through her routine in front of an enormous mirror which covered the whole wall.

I ran up to her. "Weezer!" I whispered. "Whatever's going on?"

"I'm doing my practice," she answered. "And it's Louisa, thank you very much."

"Shh," I said. "Keep your voice down. It's only six o'clock. Everyone's asleep. Come back to the room. Surely you can do your practice there?"

Weezer looked at me as though I was completely stupid. "Everyone isn't asleep," she said. "I'm not, and neither are you. So there!"

She lifted her leg straight up in front of her and bent over to touch her pointed toes. "And," she added, "this mirror's excellent. I saw it when we got out of the lift last night. And there's a barre that's just the right height. Look!"

I hadn't noticed it before. She was right. There was a sort of smooth metal railing running along one side of the corridor.

"Why d'you think it's there?" I asked. "They didn't put it there just for you to use as a barre for your ballet practice."

"Silly old them, then!" said Weezer, making sure her knees were properly turned out and checking her arm position. "I'm going to use it for that every day."

"Weezer," I said. "You can't. You'll get into trouble. I'm sure you're not allowed to treat a corridor in a posh hotel as your private practice room."

"*Louisa*," Weezer sighed. "I don't see why not. I'm not getting in anyone's way. I'll only be practising while everyone's still asleep."

I watched my sister going through her routine and tried to think of some objections to what she was saying, and I couldn't think of a single one. I was just about to leave her to it and go back to our room when a door opened a little way down the corridor and a man came out and started walking towards us.

"Weezer!" I whispered. "Look! Someone's coming . . ."

He was a chubby man, and he was wearing swimming trunks and a shirt with pineapples and leaves and red birds printed all over it. He also had a straw hat on, even though he was indoors.

"Hello, girls!" he said, in a very friendly way.

"You're not American," Weezer said.

"Don't be so cheeky!" I hissed at her.

"That's because I'm British," the man said. "Like you, it seems. I'm just going down to the pool for a dip before breakfast. Chaz Webster's my name."

"I'm Annie Blair," I said, "and this is my sister Wee– Louisa."

"Delighted to meet you," Mr Webster said, and pressed the button to call the lift. "I expect we shall meet again if you make a habit of getting up so early."

"I don't get up early at home," said Weezer, "but I have to practise every day because I'm a ballet dancer and this is the best time to do it, when everyone else is asleep."

Mr Webster stared at her. "A ballet dancer, eh?" he said. "You may be just what I'm looking for . . ."

Just then, the big silver doors opened wide and Mr Webster waved at us as he stepped into the lift.

"He's gone," Weezer said. "What d'you think he meant, about me being just what he's looking for?"

"I don't know," I said. "He probably just said it, that's all."

Weezer did her pliés, and then let go of the silver rail.

"I've finished practising," she said. " Let's go back to the room now."

I could see that she was busy wondering to herself what Mr Webster had meant, and imagining all sorts of fantastic things. I was wondering when we were going to have breakfast. My tummy knew that it was really lunch time.

Chapter Three

Later that morning we went for a drive in our hired car. I hadn't ever seen anything like Florida, except in a film. The sky was much bluer than anything I'd ever imagined, and there were palm trees lining some of the roads. The sea was bright turquoise and the beach looked like something in an advertisement. I kept saying "Weezer, look at that!" and "Dad, what's that?" and craning my neck so that I didn't miss anything as we drove along. We were going to see some dolphins that did all sorts of tricks, and I was really looking forward to it.

"I can't wait to see those dolphins, can you?" I said to Weezer, because she was being very quiet for her, and I wanted to see if she was sulking or just thinking. Sometimes it's hard to tell, and even though I couldn't think of anything in particular she might have to sulk about, you never knew with Weezer.

"Mmm," she said, which meant that she wasn't really listening to what I asked her. Then she said, "What time is it at home?"

"It's about three o'clock," said Dad.

So that was it! I suddenly realised why Weezer was so silent. She was thinking about the dress rehearsal for the dancing display, which was probably going on at this very moment, back home. All her friends would be gathering in the hall of Forest Lawn School to go over their routines for the last time.

They'd be taking their costumes from the rails where they were hanging, and getting dressed and putting on lipstick and powder. Phoebe and Tony and the others would be feeling that fluttering in their stomachs that Weezer had often tried to explain to me.

"It's like nothing else in the world, Annie," she'd say. "It's being scared and being excited and being thrilled and happy all at once. I can't describe it properly, but it's the very best feeling in the whole world."

"Better than having everyone clapping for you at the end? Telling you how wonderful you are?"

Weezer had to think about that for a moment, but in the end she said, "Yes, it's even better than that. Or maybe they're equal. I don't know, Annie."

Weezer was a very strange person. Here we were, in a place that was golden with sunshine and full of gorgeous things like swimming pools and shopping malls with all sorts of wonderful stuff in them and all she could think about was home.
I just couldn't understand it.

The dolphins were amazing. Even Weezer thought so. She took photos of everything, and got really excited when one dolphin leaped up right in front of where she was sitting. She bought postcards for Mum and Tony and Phoebe and her other friends and Mrs Posnansky, and as soon as we got back to the hotel she was all ready to write them.

"Leave them till later," Dad said. "Don't you want a swim in that pool? I can't believe you've forgotten about it already."

"I hadn't forgotten," said Weezer. "I was going to come down after I'd done them. But if we don't send them today, we'll get home before they arrive. It won't take long. I'll be there in a minute. I've only got a few to do. Are you coming too, Annie? You can write the one for Mum if you like."

"Oh, wowsers, Annie!" said Weezer as we stepped out into the sunshine beside the pool. "Isn't it fantastic? I love it! Can you see Dad?"

"Yes, there he is, on a sun-lounger – can you see? He's talking to someone . . . I don't know who it is."

We walked all round the edge of the pool till we got to where Dad was, and then we saw who it was he was chatting to. It was Mr Webster!

"Hello, girls," said Dad. "I think you've met Mr Webster, haven't you?"

"Hi, kids!" said Mr Webster.

Weezer scowled. She hates being called a kid.

Dad continued. "Mr Webster was telling me–"

"Call me Chaz," said Mr Webster. "Everyone does, young and old."

"Chaz, then," said Dad, "was just telling me that you've met before. He says you were doing your ballet practice in the corridor, Louisa."

Weezer's face was getting ready to look furious, I could see. So could Dad. He said quickly, "I don't see any reason to stop you, if that's what you want to do."

Weezer was all smiles again. "I only thought of it when I woke up early," she said. "I thought it would be all right. And I didn't want to wake you up to tell you. And then we went to see the dolphins and they were so ace and I forgot."

"That's fine," said Dad. "I don't mind. Mr– Chaz was most impressed with your dedication to ballet. He's a film director."

Weezer's mouth fell open and her eyes widened. "A film director?"

I could see she couldn't believe her ears.

"Well, in a small sort of a way. I'm here filming a commercial for Daydream Chocolates."

"I *love* Daydreams," said Weezer, and it was true. She wasn't just saying it to impress Chaz.

"I'm glad to hear that," said Chaz, "and as I've been telling your dad, I think Daydreams are going to love you. How would you like to be in a TV commercial? Both of you.

I'm filming tomorrow, down on the beach. We're making some films on a holiday theme. Tomorrow I'm filming 'Summer Daydreams'. I reckon a couple more kids leaping about with the ones we've already got will be terrific, and it might be fun for you to see how the ads you see on TV are made. Good experience if you're going to be in show business."

Weezer was so overcome that she couldn't speak. This doesn't happen to her often, so I spoke for her.

"That sounds brilliant! We'd love to come, if you really mean it. Will we be in a real, proper commercial?"

"Well, yes," said Chaz. "Even though you never really know with television . . . a lot gets shot and most of it ends up on the cutting-room floor, but there's a good chance you might be on the finished film. We start early, though, so that it's not too busy and crowded down on the beach. Eight o'clock, please."

"I'll bring them down," said Dad. "Don't worry. And is it all right if I stay and watch?"

"Oh, sure," said Chaz. "No problem at all. I'll see you right down there." He pointed. The beach was just on the other side of a road that ran past the hotel. We couldn't see it properly because there was a trellis covered in lots of leaves between the pool area and the road, but we knew where he meant.

"What shall we wear?" asked Weezer.

"What you have on right now will be fine."

Chaz got up off his sun-lounger and smiled at Dad and at us. "See you tomorrow, people!" he said, and shuffled off, his flipflops making a slapping noise on the tiles around the pool. Weezer ran to the side and did a graceful dive into the blue water.

"Come on, Annie!" she called to me when she surfaced. "It's fantastic!"

Chapter Four

Weezer got up specially early to do her ballet practice the next day, because she wanted to have time to shower and also to get me to do her hair in a special French braid. I was still asleep when she came back to the room but I soon woke up when she shook me by the shoulder.

"Come on, Annie!" she said. "We're due on the beach in an hour. You won't have time to do my hair. Get up!"

"Go away!" I said. "Go and shower. I'll get up while you're in there, I promise."

I waited until I heard Weezer turning the shower off, and then I jumped out of bed and pulled on my swimming costume. I was brushing my hair when Weezer came back, wrapped in a towel.

"Aren't you doing anything special with your hair?" she asked.

"No," I said. "We're only going to be in a crowd. Nobody's going to be filming us. Not properly. We're extras."

Weezer sniffed. She was so used to thinking of herself as the star of everything she appeared in, that she was probably dreaming of being the main person in the commercial. The new face of Daydream Chocolates, or something.

"You mustn't be disappointed if we're not in the commercial, Weezer," I said. "It's only because Chaz likes us that he's asked us to join in. We're not going to be stars, you know. Remember he said that a lot of the shots end up on the cutting-room floor . . ."

"I bet we *are* in it, though. We *could* be . . . You don't know."

She was dressed by now, and she picked up her hairbrush and turned to me. "Are you ready, Annie? I want a really gorgeous hairstyle. See if you can plait in my pink scarf with the hair. That'd be so-o-o cool."

I laughed. Weezer had only been in America for two days and already she was speaking with a bit of an accent.

"OK, OK," I said, and then suddenly I remembered. Today was the day of the dancing display. The thought of being in a TV commercial had made Weezer forget all about it. Wonders would never cease!

Weezer and I walked across the white sand. Dad had gone to stand with some other parents, who were watching what was going on from under the shade of a sort of awning that had been put up on the beach. "Look at all the people, Annie," she said. "There are hundreds of them!"

"Well, maybe about fifty," I said, but she was right. A crowd of girls dressed in every imaginable kind of swimming costume were gathered on the sand, just beside some palm trees.

Chaz was there, in his flipflops and hat, but today he had a different shirt on. This one was covered in white sailing ships and pink sharks on a blue background. The girls were giggling in little groups. Some other men were milling around telling the girls where to go and what to do. I was just wondering how to let Chaz know that we'd arrived when Weezer bounded up to him and actually pulled at his shirt. I would never have dared to do that, and I could see that some of the other girls thought she was being really cheeky.

"We've arrived, Chaz!" she said

and smiled her very best smile.

"Oh, right! Louisa and Annie . . . right. Let's see now . . . I think you girls should be in the group over there to the left. If you go and stand over there, near that tree, then I'll let you know what you have to do in a minute."

I didn't know what to say to the crowd of girls that Chaz had put us with, but I needn't have worried. Weezer smiled her best smile and said, "Hello, we're on holiday here from England, and Chaz has invited us to join in the filming. I'm Louisa, and this is my sister Annie."

"I just love the way you speak," said one girl. "Say something else. It's neat!"

"What shall I say? I think Florida is ace!" Weezer said, and all the girls crowded round her and started chatting away as though they'd been friends for ages.

"I'm going to be a ballerina when I grow up," she told them.

"Who did your hair?" one girl asked.

"My sister," said Weezer. "She's very

artistic."

The group of girls all turned to look at me, and smiled. I smiled back. It was hard to be shy when they were all so friendly. One of them said, "I guess you talk like Louisa, don't you?"

"Yes," I said. "Though not quite as much as she does."

Just then Chaz started shouting instructions through a megaphone and we all turned to look at him. The filming was about to begin.

At first it was quite exciting, having people shouting at us.

"OK, Group A girls . . . run down to the water, and smile all the time . . . that's it . . . smile. Don't forget to smile . . . you're happy! You're dreaming of Daydreams . . . that's it! Jump! Skip!"

I could see that Weezer was really enjoying herself, but after we'd done it six times, I got fed up with being shouted at, and began to wish we'd never met Chaz.

Being in a film was boring and exhausting. I was hot and sweaty and the sunhat I was wearing was getting more and more uncomfortable and tight round my head.

But Weezer was amazing. She was enjoying whatever she was asked to do, and she was trying really hard. Everyone else was just running, but Weezer was pointing her toes, and holding out her arms and even if no one else realised what was going on, I knew that in her own head, Weezer was the star of the show; the one the camera must be pointing at all the time.

While Chaz went over it with them yet again, I decided that no one would notice if I was there or not, so I went to sit under a palm tree all by myself.

"Here you go, kid," said a young woman. "Have a Daydreams bar. You look as though you could do with one."

"Thanks!" I said. We'd had to hurry through our breakfast, and I was hungry. No one had said anything about lunch. I had just peeled off the wrapper when Chaz spotted me.

"Annie!" he called. "Come over here! We're about to do another take . . . come on, run!"

I ran towards him, trying to look enthusiastic. My chocolate bar was going to get all squishy in the sun if I didn't eat it soon.

By the time we'd run to the water one more time and then back again, it would probably have melted all down my arm. I took a bite of it as I ran, and then another. I must have looked very peculiar, running and eating at the same time.

"Perfect!" Chaz shouted, after we'd raced up and down the beach a couple more times. "It's a wrap!"

Weezer sank down beside me, and her head flopped on to her knees. "Phew!" she said. "Do you know what that means . . . it's a wrap? That means he's happy with the commercial now. It's finished."

"I knew that," I said, even though I didn't really. Weezer picks up a lot of stuff like this from magazines. There aren't a lot of ballet magazines, so she reads about films and acting and pop music instead.

"Did you see what I was doing, Annie? I'm sure the camera must have caught it – I did the special run that Miss Matting showed us when we ran on to the stage for the Little Swan dance . . . did you notice me?"

"Yes, it was great," I said.

"Really? You're not just saying that?"

"No, it was fine. Truly."

Chaz's voice came to us over the megaphone. "You've all done brilliantly, girls. Thanks so much. Now, if you come over to the catering wagon, there are hot dogs and popcorn for everyone. And free Daydreams bars, of course."

We took ages getting off the beach because Weezer insisted on swapping addresses with all the girls we'd been working with, so we had to go and find Dad and borrow his pen and ask one of the crew for a bit of paper. The other girls took down our address as well, and said they'd write. Weezer kept waving to them as we walked back to the Flamingo Palace.

The days went by very quickly after that. We swam in the pool, and bought little presents for everyone back home, and visited all kinds of wonderful places, and by the time we were ready to fly to London, Weezer was quite sad to be leaving.

"Aren't you longing to see the video of the dancing display?" I said to her.

"Of course I am, silly!" she said to me. "But it was a lovely holiday, wasn't it?"

"The best," I said.

Chapter Five

Weezer phoned Phoebe almost as soon as the plane touched down, and on our very first night back she went round to Phoebe's house to watch the video of the dancing display. When she came home, she looked annoyed.

"It was really good," she said.

"Why do you look so cross, then?" I asked.

"I don't know. I think I wanted it to be . . . well, not as good as it would've been if I'd been in it. But Phoebe danced really well . . ."

"I expect if you'd been in it you'd have been just as good," I said, and Weezer started to frown. "Or maybe even better." The frown vanished, and she smiled.

"I would've been, wouldn't I?" she asked.

"Definitely," I said. I changed the subject then, because we'd been talking about nothing else except the display for ages. "D'you think Chaz will remember to send us a tape of the film?" I said.

"Oh, yes," said Weezer. "I made him promise. And I wrote our address on a special card and gave it to him. I'm sure he won't forget."

"Even if he does," I said, "they'll run the advert on TV next spring. He said so, didn't he?"

"I couldn't bear to wait that long," said Weezer.

The video arrived at the end of October. Weezer was getting seriously frustrated by the time it came, and was threatening to write to Chaz and ask him what had happened, but as soon as the postman delivered it, she forgot how she had been feeling, and hugged it to her chest.

"Oh, Annie, it's here!"

"Let's put it on," I said, "and see if we're in it. Don't get your hopes up, though. Remember all that stuff about the cutting-room floor."

Weezer clutched the package even tighter. "No. I'm going to ask Phoebe and Tony and Mrs Posnanksy to come and watch it with us. We'll have a special Daydreams party. Mum said we could ages ago, when we came back from Florida. I'm going to phone them and see if they can come round this evening."

"But how can you bear to wait until this evening? Can't we just have a quick look now and then play it again when they come?"

"No we can't," said Weezer. "I'm going to give it to Mum now, so

that we can't get at it. It'll be much more fun if we all watch it together. Wait and see."

Weezer had drawn the curtains to make the room really dark, just like a cinema. Mrs Posnansky was on the best chair, and Mum and Phoebe and Weezer were on the sofa. Tony and I were on the floor on cushions and Brad the cat was in his usual spot.

"Right!" said Weezer. "It's ready now!"

It had been ready for hours. Weezer had put biscuits out on plates in the kitchen, and Mum had laid out cups and saucers for her and Mrs Posnansky, and glasses for us. We decided to watch the video before we did anything else.

Weezer pressed the remote control and the screen was filled with flashing bits of black and white and all sorts of numbers.

"It'll start in a minute," said Weezer. "Don't worry."

Weezer squeaked a bit when she saw the beach and the palm trees, and caught a glimpse of our hotel, but mostly we watched the commercial in silence. There was the crowd of girls, and a voice singing the Daydreams song, and a shot of the waves coming in to the beach and then –

"Look!" said Tony. "It's Annie! Look!"

And there I was, eating my Daydreams bar and running down the beach. The camera followed me for what seemed like ages.

"That was when Chaz called me back to

the filming," I gasped. "I was eating a Daydreams bar . . . I didn't realise they were filming me then. Oh, wow!"

"Play it again, Weezer!" Mum said as soon as it was over. "We'll know we have to watch out for Annie this time."

"What about me?" Weezer wailed. She was so upset not to have seen herself on the commercial that she didn't even notice Mum hadn't called her Louisa. "They can't have left me on the cutting-room floor, can they?"

"Let's run the tape again," said Tony. "We'll watch more carefully this time."

We looked at it again, and then three more times.

Then suddenly Tony yelled, "There! I've got it! Give me the remote and I'll freeze the frame."

We wound the tape back and played it in slow motion, and Tony pressed the button on the remote. There, sure enough, was Weezer, right at the edge of the screen, almost lost in a crowd of other girls.

"Yes!" she shouted. "It *is* me! There's the scarf you gave me, Mrs Posnansky. Annie plaited it into my hair. Look!"

Mrs Posnanksy nodded. "It is hard, but I see now. It is you, Louisa, without a doubt! Very elegant indeed! But I fear you will not from this have a career in the films, my dear. We must leave it to Annie to be . . . how do you say? A movie star. And you, you must still practise for to be ballerina."

I could see that Weezer was wondering whether to be upset or not. Suddenly, she burst out laughing.

"It's funny, isn't it? When you think of how many times we went through it, and how hard I tried . . . and I'm not even in it properly. I think it's dead funny! I don't mind, though. Because I'm a ballet dancer and they don't star in TV commercials, do they, Mrs Posnansky?"

Mrs Posnansky agreed that they did not.

"Then let's see Annie again," said Weezer. "You look brilliant, Annie! You're a star! And just think, everyone in the whole country will see you on television next year. You'll be famous. I'll have a famous sister! Three cheers for Annie!"

Sometimes my little sister can be really nice.

Red Fox Ballet Books

The perfect read for budding ballerinas!

Little Swan by Adèle Geras

Louisa has just started ballet lessons and she's
determined to be top of the class. So when
performance time comes, she knows there is only one
role for her – prima ballerina (or else!).

£2.99   ISBN 0 09 921822 4

Louisa's Secret by Adèle Geras

Louisa's new neighbour is great. There's only
one problem – he's a boy, and boys and ballet
don't mix, or do they?

£2.99   ISBN 0 09 921832 1

Louisa in the Wings by Adèle Geras

When a famous Russian ballet company comes to town,
Louisa just has to see them. Can she get the money for the
tickets in time? Or is the show destined to go on without her?

£2.99   ISBN 0 09 921842 9

A Rival for Louisa by Adèle Geras

Phoebe's new to the ballet class and Louisa
takes an instant dislike to her – she's pretty, posh and
worst of all, a good dancer, too! Can they learn to put
their differences aside and become friends?

£2.99 ISBN 0 09 921852 6